The Town Mouse and the Country Mouse

Fairy Tale Classics
STORYBOOK

This is the story of two mice, one who lived in the busy, bustling city full of buildings—he was the Town Mouse— and one who lived on a farm, near fields and forests—she was the Country Mouse.

There came a day when the Country Mouse decided she was tired of the farm.

"Nothing but cows and chickens and sheep," she said. "All my duties and chores—no fun at all."

Near a stream in the meadow, the Country Mouse dreamed about the city. She thought about all the buildings, the shops, restaurants and theaters. Life would be so much more exciting in the city, imagined the Country Mouse, who did not notice the natural beauty that surrounded her.

Meanwhile, in the heart of the city, the Town Mouse looked down from a window, wishing he could get away from the noise of cars and people, wishing instead for trees and streams and rolling hills. It must be so peaceful in the country, thought the Town Mouse.

Then the Town Mouse had an idea. He wrote a letter to his friend, Country Mouse. "Would you like to come to the city?" he wrote with his pen. "I would like to visit the countryside. Perhaps we can trade homes for a week?"

The Country Mouse thought it was an excellent idea.

The very next day the Country Mouse boarded a train which chugga-chug-chugged her from the country to the city. "I can hardly wait," she told the train conductor.

The Town Mouse did the same thing, leaving his place in the city for the rustic home of Country Mouse.

But things did not turn out as planned. On his first day in the country, the Town Mouse was frightened by a large black and white cow, bothered by bugs and bored with nothing much to do.

At night in the country, the Town Mouse was bothered by the bright light of a full moon which shined through the bedroom window. "Would someone tell those crickets to stop their racket?" he grumbled to himself, trying to cover his ears.

Things were hardly better for the Country Mouse. She couldn't stand the noise of so many cars and buses with their rumbling engines, loud horns and stinking fumes. "HONK!" "Watch out, mouse!" "Beep-beep!" "Zoooom!" — poor Country Mouse covered her ears and coughed. "Cough-cough-cough!"

So before the week was over, the Town Mouse and the Country Mouse returned to their real homes sooner than they had planned. The Town Mouse was happy again scooting along the city sidewalks on his old skateboard. The Country Mouse found pleasure in watering her pretty plants and flowers.

Both mice agreed: "There's no place like home."